Bendy-Wendy

Written by JoJo Thoreau

Illustrated by Kristina Z. Young

Little Hands Press™

MAINE, USA

Little Hands Press
70 Patterson Ridge Rd.
Thorndike, ME 04986

www.littlehandspress.org

First Edition: 2014

ISBN-13: 978-0-615-99020-0
ISBN-10: 0-615-99020-7

Library of Congress Control Number: 2014940168

1 2 3 4 5 6 7 18 17 16 15 14

Cover and interior text design by ENC Graphic Services

Printed in Malaysia

DEDICATION

Getting your first book published is a daunting task, and even more so when you're only nine years old with just a pen, a piece of paper, and a dream...

I would like to dedicate my first book to some wonderful people that have helped make my dream a reality through their support, inspiration, and generosity.

My family: For always believing in me and encouraging me to reach for the stars (no matter how high in the sky they are). A special thanks to my big brother, who is truly my first best friend in life.

Belfast Public Library: For being my favorite Friday afternoon hangout! Thank you, Jane Thompson, for making our library visits so enjoyable and introducing me to the amazing magic sitting on the library shelves.

Kristina Z. Young: For breathing life into my first book character, Bendy-Wendy. Your talented art work is only surpassed by your generosity and loving spirit.

Eddie Vincent, ENC Graphic Services: For introducing me to Kristina Z. Young (the best illustrator ever!) and for helping me through the preparation stages of publishing.

And a big thanks to the writers willing to offer time from their busy schedules to read a story from a nine year old writer with just a pen, a piece of paper, and a dream; Lynn Plourde, Chris Enss, Nancy Plain, Joanne Sundell, and Alice Duncan.

You have all given me the chance to inspire other young writers to follow their dreams and never give up.

Dream ~ Believe ~ Inspire

ADVANCE PRAISE FOR BENDY-WENDY

"*Bendy-Wendy* is a whimsical, fun and nimble read. Her tale will contort its way into your heart with remarkable agility."

—Chris Enss, *New York Times* bestselling author

"A story filled with delightful word play and energy--reading it made ME want to do a triple-flippy-floppy!"

—Lynn Plourde, Award Winning Author

"This rhyming story, by JoJo Thoreau, is a true delight. With humor and charm, it presents the predicament of a young gymnast who has hurt her back. Will she ever return to the sport she loves? Sports-minded kids will love *Bendy-Wendy*."

—Nancy Plain, Award Winning Author

"These fun pages are filled with plot bends and twists sure to touch the imagination of even the *Cat in the Hat!* Dr. Seuss fans will applaud. Mother Goose fans will fall in love with the lyrical magic of JoJo Thoreau's poetry and prose. Braver than *Brave*, cooler than *Frozen*, JoJo is a little author to watch grow into a big talent!"

—Joanne Sundell, author of the *Watch Eyes Trilogy*

Wendy is very bendy.
Perhaps the
bendiest-Wendy
ever!

She can bend forward, and backward,
she can bend to and fro. . .
She can even bend all the
way around to tickle her toe!

Wendy's little brother, Kendy, always tries to do what she does.

But when it doesn't work he likes to pretendy
That he needs to take a trip to the docs!

Bendy-Wendys must practice every day,
That must be how they can bend in every way.

But something went wrong for Bendy-Wendy one day,
And she wondered if she had finally bent the wrong way. . .

Poor Wendy had an awful pain right in the middle of her back!

How would she ever be bendy-againdy
With this pain even bigger than her other brother, Zack!

Bendy-Wendy's Mom took her to the doc
To have him check that very sore spot.

"No bendy for Wendy till it's all healed up" said the doc when they got there.
Not-so-bendy-Wendy sobbed... "That is just totally, and absolutely, not fair!"

What was Bendy-Wendy to do?? No bendy for Wendy
Would make her . . . . .

Well . . . Just "Wendy" and that would not do!

Ice packs, and heat packs,
and brothers who tease . . .
Not-so-bendy Wendy
wanted her back to heal fast . . .
"Please!"

Not so Bendy-Wendy
didn't know what to do.
No fun and no bending —
— and now a cold, too?!
Achoo!

Oh, what was she to do? She couldn't even put on her own shoe!

So there she lay, on her bed at home… "Oh!" she said,
"I can call my friends," and she picked up the phone.

But one call, two calls, three calls, four...
Not one single friend was home — **What a bore!**

Pictures on her shelf, rice bags on her bed
Wendy looked around her room with complete boredom and dread!

No friendies, and no bendies, Wendy sure felt cursed.
How could this week possibly get any worse?

Then it started to rain . . .

Sigh . . . oh, what a pain! (In her back, and in her brain!)

But wait! What was that she heard?
SHHH...don't say a word —

Clomp,
Clomp,
Clomp,

came the sounds
toward her room.
Oh no...could it be...
a witch with
a broom?

Her door creaked, and started opening… "Please not a witch!"
Wendy was hoping.

Maybe it was just her Dad, Mack. **Ugh**, nope! It was just her bothersome brother Zack— looking ready for an attack.

Zack looked across her room and spied her diary on the shelf.
"Ohhh, don't you dare!" said not-so-bendy-Wendy.
But how could she stop him herself?

She wiggled and strained with all of her might.
But she didn't think
her back would let her
get up and strike.

All of a sudden, Wendy sprung from her bed!

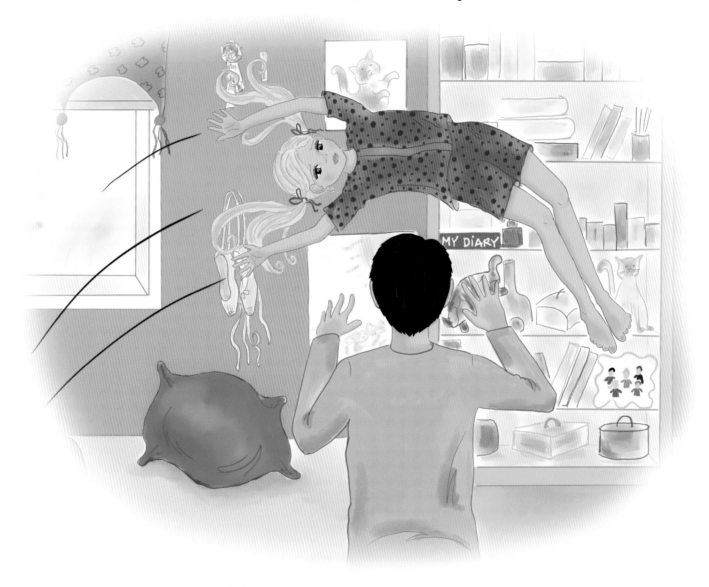

She did a triple-flippy-floppy right over Zack's head!

When her feet
hit the floor,
There was a
big POP!

But wait — there's
more...

Zack and Wendy stood still, in complete surprise.
Zack noticed the excitement in Wendy's eyes.

Do you really think…? Could it really be…?
Did that really big **POP** mean Wendy was free?

So Wendy decided to bendy — a little to and fro...
"Oh my gosh—it worked!" She could tickle her toe!

Thanks to Wendy's bothersome brother Zack,
She was able to get her back cracked back!

And now...Wendy was Bendy-Wendy againdy.

And,
perhaps,
the bendiest-Wendy
of all.

The End

About the Author

JoJo Thoreau started formulating stories when she was seven years old, and published her first book (*Bendy-Wendy*) at age nine. She lives in a rural part of Maine and loves to spend time at her local library discovering new authors as well as finding her favorites such as Dr. Seuss, Lynn Plourde, Patricia Polacco, and Chris Van Dusen. When spending time at home, JoJo Thoreau enjoys cuddle time with her kitty named Boots (hint: he looks very similar to *Bendy-Wendy's* kitty). Learn more about JoJo Thoreau by visiting littlehandspress.org. Her second book, titled *Buckaroo Bobbie Sue*, will be publishing in 2015.

About the Illustrator

Kristina Z. Young was born and raised in Zanesville, Ohio. She grew up in a house rich in art and music with her sister and brother. She was inspired by her mother who was a commercial artist and elementary teacher. Many ideas for her illustrations came from the fact that her father was a veterinarian and was constantly surrounded by dogs, cats, and farm animals. After graduating from DFMC in Texas and Kent State University in Ohio, she moved back to Texas where she met her husband. She now lives in Denton, Texas with her husband and monkey-like Brussels-Griffon dog, Hercules.